Love Notes on a Napkin

John W. Brown

ISBN 978-1-105-60225-2

The notes on each napkin were written by Sandra B. Brown. Used by permission.

Sandra, dedicated to you, the love of my life!

To our children,

Deborah, Melisa, Brooks and Natasha, Anthony and Marie,

Thanks for loving us.

And to our grandchildren,

Lily Kate, Ethan, Sydney, Peyton, and Olivia,

You are the best.

To my good friend, Katherine, thank you.

In addition, special thanks to Erica for proofreading all this mushy stuff.

Love notes on a napkin.

I have had the pleasure of officiating about 25 wedding ceremonies. During the charge of preparing each couple for their sacred bond, my desire is to say something, hopefully, that will have an effect in their relationship. To offer words of wisdom, they will use to realize a happy, fulfilling life.

A few words I hope to impress upon the couple is expressed in the following illustration:

> *Picture your marriage or relationship as a treasure chest. Consider the chest a place where you put stuff in your marriage – gifts, tokens of appreciation, souvenirs, selfless behavior, memories, dreams, and things you share. You should not make the mistake of reaching in the box, taking things out, and claiming them solely for you. Soon, your hands would be full and the box would be empty. You need to place things in the chest often. Then, keep your treasure chest or relationship full of the things you share and your hands empty. This will help create a marriage full of wonderful experiences for two loving and unselfish people.*[1]

My wife and I live by these words. We are friends and soul-mates; choosing to live our lives to the fullest; filling our treasure chest with memories; and, making each moment special. One of these special moments is opening my lunchbox and finding inside a love note. It may have something simple and sweet, yet it has exactly what I need to hear every day.

I chose 31 napkins, a month's supply of love notes, to share with you.

HAPPY WEDNESDAY

Hope today is a Great DAY for you! Two more till the Weekend, I can hardly wait to have time with you!

Love You
With All My Heart,
Body & Soul!

HAVE A
GOOD DAY

Have a good day.

Often people speak these words in passing with little thought or no intended meaning. Others can say the words and you know they mean them. Almost every day, for the past sixteen and a half years, my wife speaks to me these words: *I hope you have a good day.*

She has no clue as to what each day holds; but, she knows that by giving words of encouragement, she helps set the mood in which I face each one. Quick to give the assurance that I always have her in my corner, she desires good things to happen for me. She makes the effort, no matter how she is feeling. In part, due to her encouragement, I am more at ease, more grateful, and more successful in whatever I do.

As Elvis Costello sings,

She may be the reason I survive

The why and wherefore I'm alive

The one I'll care for through the rough in many years

Me, I'll take her laughter and her tears

And make them all my souvenirs

For where she goes I've got to be

The meaning of my life is she[2]

It feels great to have a wife, a friend, praying that you have a good day. I may experience difficulty or have a bad day, but I end up having a good day returning home to the one I love.

I love U.

She tells me *I love you* every day and shows me in so many ways. Because of this love, my life has changed forever. I am in debt to her for a lifetime.

I.O.U.

You believe that I've changed your life forever
And you're never gonna find another somebody like me
And you wish, you had more than just a lifetime
To give back all I've given you and that's what you believe

And I'm amazed when you say it's me you live for
You know that when I'm holding you, you're right where you belong
And, oh my love, I can't help but smile with wonder
When you tell me all I've done for you 'cause I've known all along

That I owe you the sunlight in the morning
And the nights of honest loving that time can't take away
And I owe you more than life now, more than ever
I know that it's the sweetest debt I'll ever have to pay[3]

BABY,
I sure miss
you ♡ Hope
today & tonight
go by fast ♡
Be careful &
Hurry home ♡
I look forward
to seeing you ♡
Love You ♡

Baby…

An expression of love two people share. One which sets their relationship apart and on a level different from anyone else in the world. People call me by my name, but only my wife reserves the right to call me *Baby.*

I sure miss you…

She misses me. When I hear these words, I know she feels the same way about me I feel about her. Constant companions for over seventeen years, she still enjoys when I am around, and feels like part of her is missing when I am not.

Hope today & tonight go by fast…

On the evenings I teach at the University of Phoenix, the day is much, much longer. When we part in the morning, it will be almost sixteen hours before I see her again. Most of the time, we act like young kids, in love, with feelings of not wanting to part company. Still, life's responsibilities demand our time and energy.

If we allowed, these things could cause us to drift apart.

But there is no worry when you know that you have someone waiting at home.

Be careful & hurry home.

When one knows they have someone waiting for them; they take extra care in returning home. I do not detour, stop at a friend's house, or go sit somewhere. I want to go home to see my *Baby* as fast as I can.

I hope you have
a good day & it goes
by quick. I miss you
very much! I can
hardly wait till we
have a vacation &
I'm well! I love my
time with you always

Love You
The Most-est P

I can hardly wait until we have a vacation…

Vacations are important to a marriage. It is a time for husband and wife to get away from the pressures of life, out from underneath the suffocating stress of work, raising children (or grandchildren and their parents), and celebrate togetherness. It is our time. We spend every moment together (except when she allows me to play golf and she goes shopping). Sometimes we have the money to take a trip; other times we have a staycation. Either way is fine with us.

I love my time with you always.

When we travel, we love taking trips by automobile. We take our time, relax, and talk all the way there. For us, spending time together means sharing. In our relationship, communication has never been a problem. We talk about everything – our children, plans, desires, dreams, everything. Every one of life's little detail; we examine and provide each other with our own perspective. Sometimes we agree; sometimes, we do not. However, it is not about agreeing all the time; it is about sharing and spending time with the one you love.

Yea it's Friday
Seems like it's been
two weeks since
you were off
Love you & hope
today is a great day
xoxoxo Love You
4-ever

Yea it's Friday...

It seems like we live just for the weekend.

While at work, I find the time to think about her. I know later, she will greet me at the door with a smile and kiss, knowing the workweek is over and now it is our time. I can hardly wait! It does not matter if our children, grandchildren, or friends come by for a visit or we have plans out of the house; weekends are our favorite time.

Love you 4-ever.

Will our love last forever? Forever is such a long time; it seems impossible to comprehend. Couples in love should have faith in each moment they share. We believe that if we are attentive in taking care of these moments, the *4-ever* will take care of itself.

Forgetting past hurts and disappointments is necessary. In our relationship, the difficulty we may have in trusting others does not matter. What is the secret? The emphasis is not placed on the conditions of the relationship. It is placed on making each moment of our lives count.

Extra fork incase
one breaks :)
Hope you enjoy ♡

Extra fork in case one breaks. Hope you enjoy.

For lunch, there is nothing better than the wife's leftover roast beef, potatoes, carrots, and green beans. The celebrated Sunday dinner, her children grew up on, and now her grandchildren ask for. Opening my lunch box and discovering these things is a *feel good* moment in the middle of the day.

She is extraordinary. She sees little details others may overlook – like an extra fork, *in case one breaks.* Often, she tells me that she does not want to take me for granted. Yet, in so many ways, she is careful to show me the smallest considerations. I should be the one more responsible in caring for and considering her needs and desires.

Hi BABY, Hope
your interview
went well & hope
you get the job
if that's what you
want ♡ I love you
& pray for the Best
for you ♡ You
deserve the best ♡
Love You Sweet Heart
Be careful & hurry home
XOXOXO

My wife sees through all my frustrations and disappointments. When I am down, she is a dependable source of encouragement. I am continually aware she prays for me and this serves as a reminder that God is my highest source of strength. She, not only prays for the things I want, she prays for what is best. She knows my heart and soul.

After graduating with an MBA, I hoped things would change quickly. However, struggling through almost two years, I was beginning to worry and doubt.

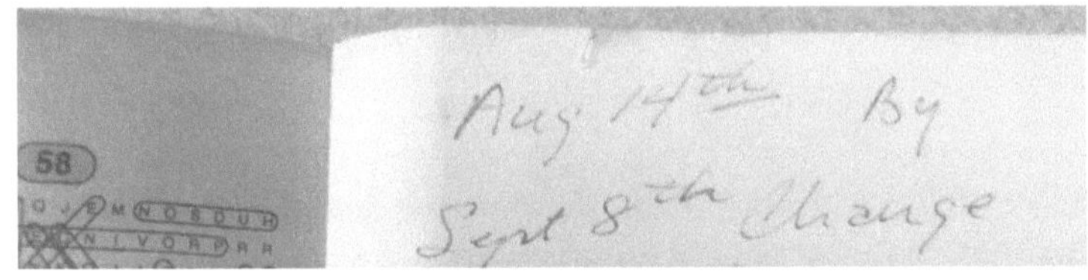

On August 14, as she worked her crossword puzzle book, she was praying for me. She had this thought that things would change for me by September 8. She turned to the last page in the book and wrote the date *August 14th* and then added *by Sept 8th change.* She did not know it at the time; I was discussing the prospect of pursuing another position. The next day I sent an email to the hiring manager and set up an interview on August 18.

The manager offered the position on September 7. Two days before, September 5, she let me see the hand written note in the back of the crossword puzzle book.

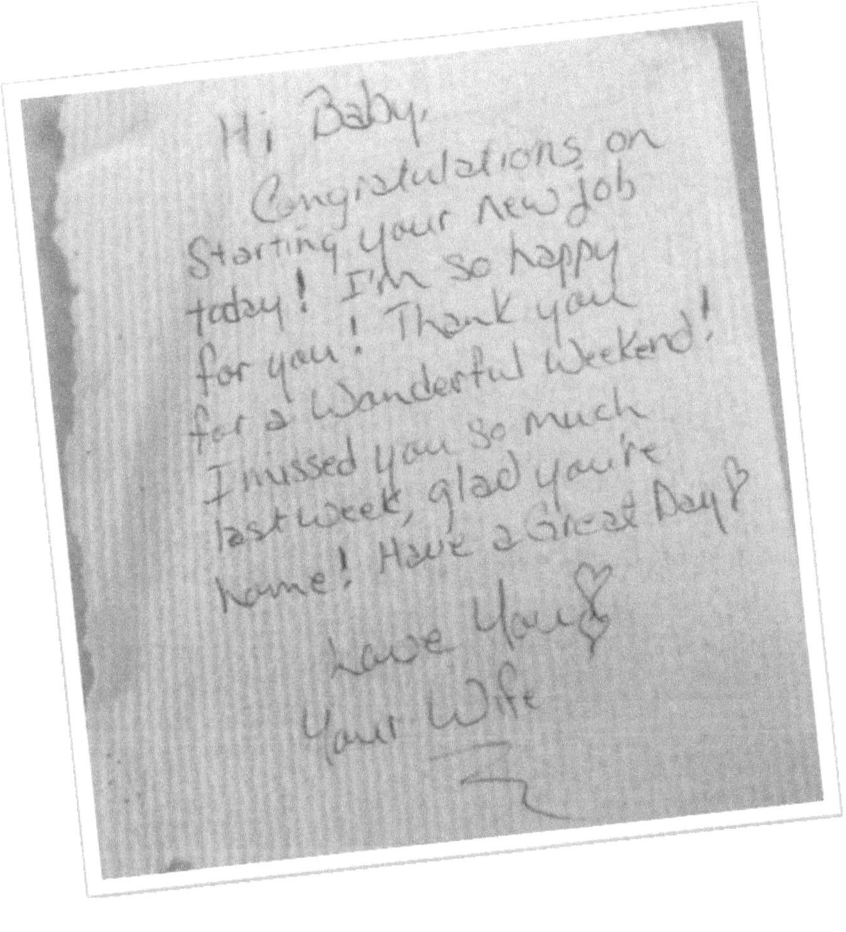

Hi Baby,
Congratulations on
Starting your new job
today! I'm so happy
for you! Thank you
for a Wonderful Weekend!
I missed you so much
last week, glad you're
home! Have a Great Day!

Love You!
Your Wife

Hi Baby,

So glad your home from the trip. You are my world & I am so happy for you in your new job! HAVE A GREAT DAY! LOVE You ♡

XOXOXO

Hi Baby!
Hope you enjoy
your lunch!
I LOVE You
With ALL MY
HEART
HAVE A GREAT
DAY

Hope you enjoy your lunch…

During the workday, I miss her the most at lunchtime. Working for the same company, we were privileged to spend this time together. Unfortunately, it changed after she went on disability. We lived only seven minutes away, so I would go home for lunch. However, someone strongly suggested I have lunch in the workplace cafeteria, along with my peers and leadership. I complied; but, my heart was home.

I still miss her. So, I decided that during lunchtime, I would take all of these napkins, write a little about our love, and create this book.

I love you with all my heart.

These are compelling, gargantuan words. When she says the words *I love you*, it is with singleness and sincerity. I cannot deny it; these words overwhelm me with joy and happiness. She belongs to me; not as a possession, her heart is simply mine.

BABY,
I miss you so
much & So glad
tomorrow is Friday &
I'll have 2 days with
you ♡ Hope today is
a good one ♡ Hurry
home & be careful ♡
LOVE You

XOXOXOXOXOXOXOXO

XOXOXOXOXOXOXO

Hugs and Kisses! Our children playfully tease us about the affection we show one another. They say we make them sick because we kiss goodbye, even if we are just running to the store. We say *I love you* often. We hold hands, compliment each other, say encouraging words, and always look into one another's eyes to communicate we understand. Our love and affection keeps us in tune as a couple.

We talk, laugh, share, and visit with others; yet the small, tender affections we show each other separate our relationship from all others. And the exciting part, we enjoy discovering new ways to express our love and affection.

YEA IT'S
FRIDAY!
Hope you have
a Good Day!
Love You
SweetHeart

Often used thoughtlessly by others, this term of endearment expresses the temperament of our relationship. To be sweet to one another is our most sincere desire. When I need a kind, encouraging word, my wife is the first to give. She has the ability to anticipate my anxieties and fears and offer something constructive and positive.

Our home is peaceful and safe because we live and practice pleasantries. There are no enemies in this house. This does not mean we agree on every issue. Sometimes, we find ourselves on opposite sides. However, we do not look at each other as rivals. We trust one another and always work together for a positive outcome.

Her mother, Marie, cultivated this quality of sweetness in Sandra's heart. She and her sister were caregivers to their mom for more than twenty years. Marie harbored no ill will toward anyone; she lived as a lady free of bitterness or hate. Once asked if when she arrives in heaven, would she ask God why He allowed her to live life as an invalid? She replied, *No, because it won't matter then.*

HI BABY!
I Love You
the Most-est!!!

I love you the most-est!!!

I love the way she loves me! Investing her heart and soul in knowing me, she looks beyond all my faults and loves me anyway.

We struggled the first few years of marriage with baggage brought from previous relationships. Neither of us wanted the memories of bad experiences to destroy the peace and happiness we shared. So, we resisted the feelings of pain and failure by talking to one another.

In addition, we learned that knowing how to talk to one another is just as important as doing it. Sometimes, I had difficulty trusting her words or actions. There were times she would test my love and fortitude. Still, we resolved to talk through our difficulties.

Our motto is the same today as it was in the beginning - friends first.

One thing that bothers me, we have one continuous source of conflict – she believes she loves me more than I love her.

I CAN HARDLY
WAIT TO SEE
YOU
LOVE YOU
the MOST-EST!!!

I can hardly wait to see you.

In his song, Got My Heart Set on You, John Denver sang the words, *"baby every time I see you, before I even leave you I can hardly wait to see you again."*[4] This is how my wife and I feel every time we part company. During the time in between, it is like a child's excitement and anticipation of Christmas.

It is not always about a night of romance. We get excited about watching our favorite entertainment shows of the season – *American Idol*, *Big Brother*, or the *Housewives of New Jersey*. On the other hand, we may look forward to eating dinner, sitting on the sofa, talking about our day, and retiring early to bed. Whatever the evening holds, we know the most important thing is to be together at the end of the day.

Happy Thursday Baby,
One more day yea!
I love you with
all my Heart, Body
& Soul ♡ Hope
today goes by fast
& your foot gets well!
See you soon, be
careful & hurry home!
Love You ♡

I love you with all my heart, body, and soul.

Since the beginning of our marriage, we have made this statement. It represents the completeness of our love. We give each other *heart, body, and soul* and with this, there is the confidence we belong together.

I shared with a nursing supervisor the idea of this book. After reading a few napkins, Katherine stated, *"There's no reason you should turn your head to look at another woman."* She is right. After all these years, my wife is the only woman who turns my head.

Hope today goes by fast & your foot gets well!

I know she cares about me. It is uncomplicated to give your heart, body, and soul to someone who loves you. Her heart represents the sensitivity and compassion she has for everyone; her body represents her energy and abilities in which she loves; and, her soul is uniquely herself. She is real, not insincere or deceitful. She is everything I want and need!

TGIF!

OH BABY I
LOVE YOU SO MUCH
AND I AM SO
HAPPY TO BE
YOUR WIFE, I LOVE
MY LIFE WITH YOU
HOPE YOU HAVE
A GREAT DAY!

XOXOXOXOXO

Married in 1995 and excited about the hope of rebuilding our lives together, we promised each other that we would be friends for life. Yet, she did not want me to call her *wife*. She acknowledged happiness in being with me and did not want to belong to anyone else. But, the issue was with the word *wife*; it made her feel like a servant.

From the baggage of her past, she quickly shared with me these fast and hard rules:

- I could not sit in my easy chair and shout at her to run into the room and hand me the remote that is on the table in front of me and get mad if she refuses to come.
- I could not sit in the same chair or on the side of the bed and ask her to hand me shoes, which are on the floor in front of me or in the same room.
- I could not stand in the middle of the living room, not really doing anything, and command her to run out to the vehicle and fetch anything I may have left there.

- If she tells me she needs something or one of our children needs something, I could not come home, grinning, and show her the stuff I bought for myself.

She learned quickly, I was not this type of man. After a few years into marriage, she began to appreciate the term *wife* again. She is not a possession, but a part of me. We serve one another and there is no screaming, yelling or threat of physical abuse if one fails to *obey* the other.

When husbands and wives are friends first, the relationship is much more meaningful. And a man should not be lazy in his relationship with his wife nor take her for granted.

Hi Baby,
Hope you're having a Great Day!
Thank you for taking care of me this weekend ♡
I miss you already!
Love You

XOXOXO

Love you Baby!
Hope you have a
Great Day!
I miss you so much!
Can hardly wait for you
to come home! Be
Careful!
Love You
the Most-est

Hi Baby,

Hope you feel better today! I Love you so much & I love life with you! Have a Great Day & I look forward to seeing you this evening

Love You,

Me (Your Wife)

I love life with you!

Reading these words make me a happy man. She has stood beside me through sixteen years of marriage. She has endured with me the shame of divorce. She waited patiently for me through years of struggling to make the right career choice; eight years for completing college degrees, while she learned to cope with a debilitating disease; and, both of us balancing the demands of four children and five grandchildren.

We are blessed. Not always taking the easy road, we have learned to take life one day at a time and appreciate God's mercies and goodness. Ray LaMontagne put into song what I sing in my heart, "*You are the best thing ever happened to me.*"[5]

Lifc is precious and we should not live it worrying about things which we cannot do anything; taking on stress that is not ours to experience; or creating issues for unnecessary fussing and fighting.

We live by this rule found in the Bible,

"For let him who wants to enjoy life and see good days [good--whether apparent or not] keep his tongue free from evil and his lips from guile (treachery, deceit)."[6]

1 Peter 3:10 (Amplified Bible)

In marriage, no words should be spoken with malicious intent, dishonesty, or betrayal of the heart.

I'm going
to miss you
today! Sorry I didn't
feel better this weekend at
least I'll be better next weekend.
I hope you have a good day!
I love you with all my
heart, body & soul ♡

Love you
Always ♡

Sorry I didn't feel better this weekend…

Although, I never said a word, she apologizes for not feeling better. Right away, I understand her meaning; we missed time together. These words are not spoken for sympathy. She does not play games with my thoughts or emotions. She feels regret that we did not do something or go somewhere together.

She loves me so much; I can wait, without frustration and anger, until she feels better. I just love being with her anytime, anywhere.

At least I'll be better next weekend.

I Sure missed you
last night & I'm so
Proud of you and love
you with all my
Heart ♡ HAVE A GREAT
DAY & Maybe it'll go
by fast ♡ Love You

XOXOXO

I'm so proud of you.

Last night was the first time teaching at the University of Phoenix. It was exciting finally to feel recognition and appreciation for years of working days and spending evenings doing schoolwork. With just a few words, my wife is there to let me know she understands my feelings and tells me how proud she is.

Pride is not always a bad thing. We can be proud of our children, our home, and each other. Vanity is never a good thing; however, a man needs to have a sense of worthiness. She knows how important this is for me. Having raised two sons, she understands men need things to be proud of and need someone to be proud of them.

Where would I be without her love and encouragement? She has made a tremendous investment in my life; and for this reason, she is a stakeholder in my success. What a wonderful thing it is: having her with me, sharing these exciting moments.

Thank You Baby
for my watch
& face treatments ♡
I love them ♡
You are an amazing
man in so many
ways ♡. Thank You
for being my husband
and my friend ♡
Love You
With All MY HEART
♡
XOXOXO

Dillard's Day at work! For our anniversary this year, we bought a new transmission for our Ford Expedition, which left a terrible feeling inside. We had planned on taking a trip to Savannah, Georgia. However, the week of my vacation, the transmission went out. So, we postponed it. This left me wondering what I was going to do for our anniversary celebration. I bought a card, a small gift, and prepared her a special evening dinner.

Three months later, my employer brought Dillard's Department store in for a fundraiser. I asked my wife if she would like to come by and check out the merchandise. She leaves with a Michael Kors watch and some Estee Lauder and I am an amazing man, thanks to the Foundation.

I Miss You already
I enjoyed the
weekend as always!
4 more Days!

Love You
The Most-est

I enjoyed the weekend as always!

As husband and wife, we have spent approximately 850 weekends together. Although, we would like to have this time together (alone sometime), life does not always cooperate.

No matter what our plans may be, life happens. From children and grandchildren dropping in for sleepovers to birthday parties, helping friends in need, work, school, sickness or having to do repairs around the house, there is always something to do.

In addition, we have opened our home to family during their times of crisis or hardship. With a full house, we still enjoy our weekends together.

We have a wonderful life. Even if, I have to sit and watch a *Twilight* movie, the *Housewives of Orange County* or *New Jersey*, or go shopping all day on Saturday, I cannot complain. The feelings are mutual. Occasionally, she *allows* me to watch the Razorbacks or play golf while she goes shopping.

Couples in love should make time for each other. Even if it is spending time with family and friends; sitting on the sofa talking after the evening is done; relaxing a few minutes before bedtime; unwinding from the weekend, no matter what the circumstances, we find every opportunity to be together.

I miss you
Hope your foot
gets better &
Stops hurting!
Love You
Sweet Heart

Hope your foot gets better & stops hurting.

As a child, I poked fun at Dad for having gout. I thought the name of the disease was hilarious. However, it is not so funny anymore, especially during the night, when my wife bumps my big toe. It is excruciating pain.

Now, I respect and praise my mother for taking care of dad during his times of illness and eventual death. Through everything, she stood by him. Sometimes, I remember a funny man who loved to laugh at himself. Other times, I remember a hard and difficult man; however, mother knew him as a man who needed love, support, and a lot of prayer.

Today, I live blessed with a wonderful wife, who is equally concerned about me. She notices everything about me. Happy, worried, or hurting, she is there. I matter to her.

Hi Baby
Hope you're
having a good
day! Thank you
for all you do!
I Love the
Bathroom! I
Miss you when
we're apart!

Love You,
Sandra
AKA. Baby

Hope you're having a good day!

Knowing it will be the middle of the day when I read this note, she anticipates my feelings and writes to let me know she listens and understands. Not just when it is convenient for her or when I say something she wants to hear; but, when I express my doubts or frustrations, she is always there for me.

She encourages me with these words on a napkin...

Thank you for all you do!

This past weekend, I bought wallpaper, paint, and trim for a bathroom she wanted remodeled five years ago. In my mind are thoughts of people still laughing at the carpentry work I did as a younger man. In spite of that, through her acknowledgement and appreciation, I have learned to be a better handyman.

Because of her encouragement, I desire to be a better man.

It's Friday!
I Love you and
miss you every day
we're apart! I'm
looking forward to the
weekend with you!

[illegible]

I'm looking forward to the weekend with you!

We created our treasure chest Friday, May 12, 1995, in front of the fireplace in my new sister and brother-in-law's apartment. Later in the evening, we drove to Hot Springs, Arkansas and stayed two wonderful nights at the Arlington Hotel. It was like heaven on earth. Of course, it helped that Sandra's cousin provided the gift of a spa package; consequently, setting the bar high for weekend excursions.

Since then, we have shared many exciting adventures. From touring our home town Little Rock, Arkansas to a Bon Jovi concert in Memphis. These escapades can be large or small; expensive or inexpensive. We choose the adventure we desire. The important thing is: we make the time for one another.

On our fifth wedding anniversary, we went back to the Arlington Hotel. During the week, we reminisced about our first five years together. Taking whatever I could to write on, we tried to recall something special we did each month (we organized it later).

- 08/13/96 - Tour of the Arkansas Territorial Restoration
- 08/17/96 - Tour of the Decorative Arts Museum
- 08/20/96 - UALR Planetarium
- 08/21/96 - Tour of the Villa Marre

#16 - September 1996
Arkansas Rep Theater - "Little Shop of Horrors"
- 09/27/96 - Section 27, Row 1, Seat 1&2
- Juanita's Mexican Restaurant - 1st time

#17 - October 1996
- Arkansas State Fair
- UCA presents "Pure as the Driven Snow"
Brianna Boyce played Nellie Morris, a woman of mystery

#18 - November 1996
- Wiederkehr Wine Cellars, Inc. in Altus, Arkansas - 11/09/96
(Took Sam with us. Stopped at the Dollar Tree in Russellville.)
- Southern Living Cooking School, Robinson Center Exhibit Hall - 11/12/96

#19 - December 1996
- Mom bought us the Entertainment Center.

#20 - January 1997
- Wayne started working for Arkansas Fidelity Mortgage Corporation.

#21 - February 1997
- *The Valentine Concert - Bill Cosby - 02/16/97*
Robinson Center Music Hall - Section: Orchestra, Row S, Seats 209 & 210

#22 - March 1997
- *First Concert - Celine Dion*
Mid-South Coliseum, Memphis, TN - 03/14/97 (Brooks & Natasha went with u
Section H-N, Row 27, Seat 1 & 2
- We ate at Bonanza in West Memphis before the concert.
- Bought 1987 Mercedes Benz from Jan

23 - April 1997
- Anthony and Marie's Wedding Day

4 - May 1997
- Eureka Springs - The Great Passion Play
- Ricky, Marie, Cil and Mom went with us.

LOVE
YOU
MR BROWN

Love you Mr. Brown

In the early years of marriage, my wife spoke a great deal about the desire not to lose her identity; and, I have been careful to show her the respect she deserves. She has a mind of her own, as well as feelings, desires, hopes, and dreams. Her children and grandchildren respect and admire her. Even the daughter-in-laws know to call her and hear *what mom would do.*

To me and others, she always shows kindness, courtesy, and respect. I am proud to be her husband.

Katherine wanted to know if my wife wrote a note after a fight or disagreement. The answer is *yes she does.* When I take my lunchbox, there is a note inside. Even when there is a disagreement, she seems to say *I may not always agree with you, but I do love and respect you.*

A few years ago, visiting my cousin and his wife in Dallas, sitting on the patio, enjoying a nice meal and a beautiful evening, my wife was talking and I squeezed her leg. Out came a cry, *Ouch that hurt!* I turned at least three shades of red, apologized and she continued to talk. I did not tell them that she had instructed me to let her know if she was talking too much or dominating a conversation (which she can). I decided then, she could talk as much as she liked. Out of respect, I try not to interrupt her (or maybe it is out of fear of embarrassment). Either way, she deserves respect.

Besides, she gave me one of the greatest compliments and most public sign of respect by taking my last name…*Love you too, Mrs. Brown!*

Hi Baby,
I miss you already!
I love my time with you!
I'm sorry for everytime
I have said or done something
that hurt you or us!
I enjoyed the weekend ♡
you are the Great-est & I
am so Thankful you're
mine ♡ I LOVE YOU
WITH ALL MY HEART ♡

XOXOXOXO

HAPPY FRIDAY
BABY!
Hope today is the
Great-est of this weeks
work days!
Looking forward to
Spending the Weekend
With you! Be careful!

Love You
THE MOST-EST

Hi Baby!
I ♥ U the
Mostest!
Hurry Home!
Love You!
Me

Notes

[1] Rev. Gary W. Johnson, Married Couple's Retreat, Hot Springs, Arkansas, 1987.

[2] Daniel Jones and Darren Hayes, Elvis Costello, *She* Lyrics, Site created by LyricsFreak, (2012), 21 December 2011, http://www.lyricsfreaks.com/e/elvis+costello/she_10100904.html.

[3] Kerry Chater and Austin Roberts, Lee Greenwood, *I.O.U.* Lyrics, 26 August 2011, www.songlyrics.com/lee-greenwood/i-o-u-lyrics/.

[4] Dobie Gray and George Reneau, John Denver, *Got My Heart Set On You* Lyrics, Site created by LyricsFreak, (2012), 26 August 2011, http://www.lyricsfreaks.com/j/.

john+denver/got+my+heart+set+on+you_20073445.html.

[5] Ray LaMontagne, *You Are the Best Thing* Lyrics, 26 August 2011, www.songlyrics.com/ray-lamontagne/you-are-the-best-thing-lyrics/.

[6] BibleGateway.com, (2012), 26 August 2011, http://www.biblegateway.com/passage/?search=1%20Peter%203:10&version=AMP.

www.ingramcontent.com/pod-product-compliance
Ingram Content Group UK Ltd.
Pitfield, Milton Keynes, MK11 3LW, UK
UKHW041918190726
13854UKWH00003B/1315

9 781105 602252